God Gave Us Family

by Lisa Tawn Bergren   art by David Hohn

WATERBROOK

For Ava and Wrenna—precious
members of *our* family!

GOD GAVE US FAMILY

Hardcover ISBN 978-1-60142-876-9
eBook ISBN 978-1-60142-877-6

Text copyright © 2017 by Lisa Tawn Bergren
Illustrations copyright © 2017 by David Hohn

Cover design by Mark D. Ford; cover illustration by David Hohn

Published in the United States by WaterBrook, an imprint of the
Crown Publishing Group, a division of Penguin Random House
LLC, New York.

WATERBROOK® and its deer colophon are registered trademarks
of Penguin Random House LLC.

The Cataloging-in-Publication Data is on file with the Library
of Congress.

Printed in the United States of America
2017—First Edition

10 9 8 7 6 5 4 3 2 1

SPECIAL SALES
Most WaterBrook books are available at special quantity
discounts when purchased in bulk by corporations, organizations,
and special-interest groups. Custom imprinting or excerpting can
also be done to fit special needs. For information, please e-mail
specialmarketscms@penguinrandomhouse.com or call
1-800-603-7051.

"Mama, how come our family
only has one kid?"

"Well, Little Pup, you're the only child we have so far, and maybe the only one we'll ever have."

"But we thank God for you.
Your arrival made us a family."

"Wally's family has eight kids! And we only get one?"

"God gave them their family," Papa said, "just as he gave us ours.
Families come in all sizes."

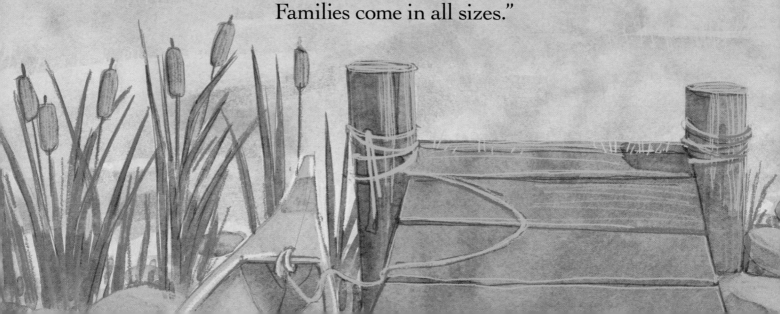

"We could 'dopt a baby," Little Pup said.

"Adopt?" Mama asked.

"Yeah. Like Ben's family."

"That's something to consider," Papa said. "It's special when a family adopts a child as their own. It's kind of like how God makes each of us a part of his family. Choosing us, loving us, forever."

"God gives us family in lots of different ways," Papa said.
"Look at Graham the Goose. His mama is raising
all those goslings by herself."

"Yeah, but they get to see their dad this summer.
He lives on another pond."

"Sometimes a mama or papa can't be a part of raising their
kids every day," Papa said. "But they're still family."

"Maxwell lives with his grampa and gramma,"
Little Pup said. "Are they a family too?"

"You bet," Mama said. "Whenever somebody is
loving and caring for another, that's a family."

"Our pack is a part of our family too," Mama said.

"*What!*" Little Pup exclaimed. "But some of 'em aren't even related to us!"

Mama smiled. "That's how God works. He brings together those who love him to create an even greater family."

"I usually like being in a pack. But sometimes they're *annoying,*" Little Pup grumbled.

"It's true. Even family can get on our nerves now and then," Papa said. "Just like we can get on theirs. But because we're family, we figure out how to get along. We need to love the family God gave us."

"*This* is all our family?" Little Pup asked.

"Yep," Papa said. "God gave us every one."

"I think I like our family best now," Little Pup whispered, "when everyone's sleepy and quiet."

"It is good, isn't it?" Mama whispered back. "But God gave us family to enjoy in quiet *and* loud times."

"Some families stay out all night,
like the raccoons!" Papa said.

"That's crazy," Little Pup said. "I'm glad God
didn't give us *that* sort of family."

Little Pup smiled when his favorite cousin finally arrived. His cousin liked to play like he did…and was good at helping him ignore the more annoying little wolves.

But then Little Pup met two new cousins and decided
he liked them too. And the three wolf pups that had
driven him crazy last year seemed better this time.
Over the next few days, they made a fort…

And played hide-and-seek…

And climbed high so they could howl at the moon…

And hung out with their
grandparents, listening
to them tell old stories…

And that night, Little Pup decided
he'd never want a different family.
He liked—no, *loved*—the one
God gave him.